This book belongs to:

A catalogue record for this book is available from the British Library

Published by Ladybird Books Ltd
A subsidiary of the Penguin Group
A Pearson Company

First published by Ladybird Books Ltd MCMXCVI   This edition MCMXCVII

LADYBIRD and the device of a Ladybird are trademarks of
Ladybird Books Ltd Loughborough Leicestershire UK

Text © Christine Morton MCMXCV
Illustrations © Nigel McMullen MCMXCV

The author/artist have asserted their moral rights

Don't Worry
William

by Christine Morton
illustrated by Nigel McMullen

Ladybird

One night, Horace and his teddy bear,
William, woke up and decided to be naughty.
They waited till Mum was snoring – *zzzzzzzz*.
Then they got out of bed. Horace jumped
into his monster slippers and the two bears
crept downstairs.

Downstairs, it was dark. Sleepy dark.
Creepy dark. In the living room, they heard
a noise. A whispery noise. A crispery noise.
Horace was scared. "Maybe it's a spook!"

"Tick-tock, tick-tock," said the noise.

"Don't worry, William," said Horace.
"It's only the clock!"

Behind the curtain, Horace heard a growl.
A small growl. A yowl-growl. Horace was
scared. "Maybe it's a lion!" he thought.

"*Mee-ow!*" said the noise.

"Don't worry, William," said Horace.
"It's only the cat."

In the kitchen, Horace heard a pop.
A soft pop. A bubbly pop. Horace was
scared. "Maybe it's a giant frog, gulping
in the dark!" he thought.

"Bob, bob, bob," said the noise.

"Don't worry, William," said Horace.
"It's only Bob the goldfish, swimming
round and round his tank."

Horace and William decided it wasn't
so much fun being naughty. They felt a bit
wobbly and worried. So they went to find
some biscuits, to make them brave.

Horace had *just* got his hands into the biscuit tin when he heard a bang. A Very Loud bang! An On-The-Stairs bang. *BANG, BANG, BANG!*

"There's a th-th-thing!" said Horace. "And it's coming downst-st-stairs!"

They hid behind the settee.

The door opened... *cree-eeak!*

And there stood...

    ...The Thing!

The Thing was big. The Thing was cross.
The Thing looked a bit like Mum!
The Thing took a deep breath and said...

"You naughty little boy! Put those biscuits down
and GET UP THOSE STAIRS AT ONCE!"

"Oh, Mum," wailed Horace.
"We thought you were a Thing."

Mum put them back to bed.
Back to their big blue bed. Back to their cosy,
dozy cabin bed with no spooky noises.
"Sorry, Mum," said Horace.

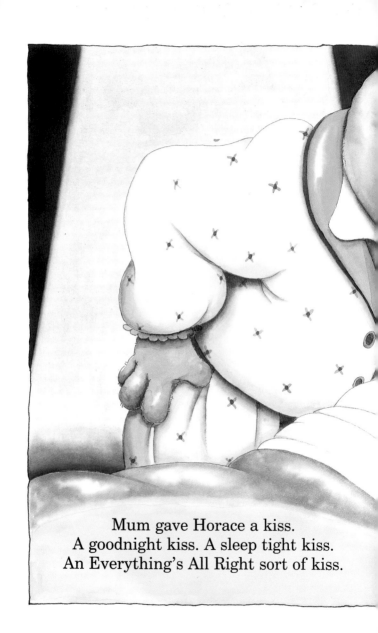

Mum gave Horace a kiss.
A goodnight kiss. A sleep tight kiss.
An Everything's All Right sort of kiss.

Downstairs, the clock went *tick-tock, tick-tock*. The cat went *mee-ow, mee-ow*. The fish went *bob, bob, bob*.

Upstairs, Horace went *zzzzzzzz*. Mum went *zzzzzzzz*. Even William went *zzzzzzzz*.

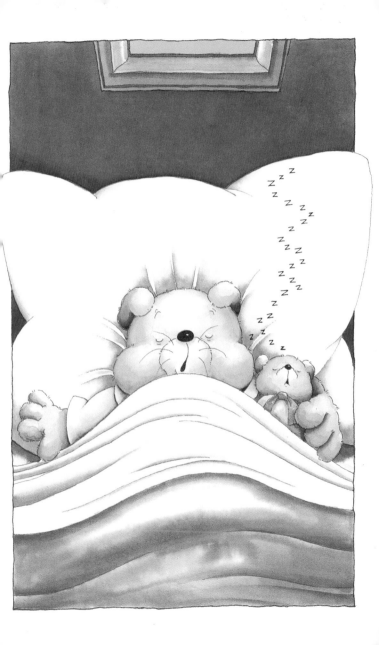

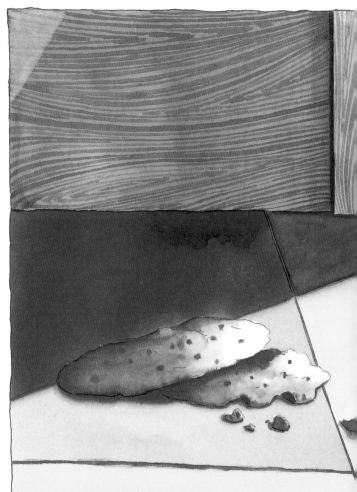

And in the kitchen, a little brown mouse
crept behind the door – and stole the biscuits.